This igloo book belongs to:

...............Tiana Rose Fusco.......

igloobooks

Published in 2014
by Igloo Books Ltd
Cottage Farm
Sywell
NN6 0BJ
www.igloobooks.com

HUN001 0514
2 4 6 8 10 9 7 5 3
ISBN 978-1-78197-630-2

Illustrated by Melanie Mitchell

Printed and manufactured in China

TIME FOR BED

igloobooks

When the sun sets in the garden and the stars start to come out,
The bunnies should be sleeping, but they're still playing about.

"Time for bed!" calls Mummy Rabbit,
standing at the door.

"Oh, we don't want to sleep!" they cry.
"We want to play some more!"

"Come inside now," Mummy says.
"It's getting very late.
Your bedtime was an hour ago
and now it's nearly eight!"

"Quick, let's run away and hide,"
the naughty bunnies say.

So giggling and squealing, all the bunnies run away.

"Here I come!" laughs Mummy Rabbit,
heading for the pool.
She scoops up little Fluffy
in a blanket made of wool.

"Come on then," says Mummy Rabbit. "It's time to get you dried."
She carries Fluffy in her arms and takes her back inside.

Soon, Fluffy had her nightclothes on
and she was nice and ready.
So Mummy said, "Goodnight,"
as Fluffy snuggled with her teddy.

She tiptoed out the room and turned
when she had reached the door,
and there was naughty Fluffy
playing on the bedroom floor!

So Mummy Rabbit tucked up Fluffy back into her bed.
She slowly shut the door and sighed. "Hoppy next," she said.

Hoppy raced around downstairs until he felt quite sick.

"That's enough," said Mummy Rabbit. "Brush your teeth. Be quick!"

Hoppy ran upstairs, but didn't brush his teeth at all.
"Go and brush your teeth, right now!" he heard his mummy call.

After Hoppy's teeth were clean,
Mummy tucked him up.
"Here's your drink," said Mummy,
giving him his little cup.

Munchy and his brother, Crunchy,
played with all their toys.

Then, Mummy came to fetch them.
"Up to bed now, naughty boys!"

They packed their toys away again. "Well done," their mummy said.
"There's no more time for playing now. It's time to go to bed."

Munchy curled up safe and warm
and snuggled with his ted.
"Goodnight, my darling," Mummy said,
while stroking Munchy's head.

Then Crunchy yawned a little yawn and whispered, "I love you."
Mummy smiled and kissed his cheek. "Goodnight. I love you, too."

Baby Bunny was the final rabbit to be found.

"Where's she hiding?" Mummy thought. "I don't see her around."

Mummy searched the whole house through.
She looked in every room.
Until, at last, she found her
in the cupboard with the broom.

Mummy laughed and scooped her up,
then kissed her happy face.
"There you are, my darling.
What a funny hiding place!"

At last, the little bunnies
were all tucked up tight in bed.

"I think it's even time for me to sleep now,"
Mummy said.

Mummy smiled at all her children,
then she shut the door.
She settled in her comfy chair
and soon began to snore.